The Sile
Knowing

Jenny Jackson

For David
and for
Nathan and Ellie Wakinshaw
with much love

Contents

Chapter 1

"We should die together," Mitch said, "seeing as how we were born together."

I nodded my agreement. Our problem was how to carry out this joint suicide. There was a can of poisonous weed killer in the garden shed but on the very highest shelf well out of our reach and besides, it would probably have made us sick before we could have swallowed enough. Drowning was out of the question due to a complete lack of suitable water. We were miles from the sea, a river or even a pond and the tin bath that hung on a hook in the outhouse wasn't deep enough to drown a cat. We thought of throwing ourselves under a bus, but what if it ran over one and missed the other? It was no use - we would have to go back to school on Monday. Our glorious summer freedom was over for another year.

"Josie! Mitch! Home - now!"

Our grandmother's voice screeched in a dead straight line across the newly reaped wheat field and up into the sturdy branches of our hiding tree. How could such a bellow come out of such a little person? Knowing better than to disobey we jumped down and ran through sharp stubble, across the dusty lane and in at the ever-open kitchen door. Our grandmother was at the stove, a cloth wrapped around the handle of the tin kettle, about to pour boiling water into the waiting teapot.

"Wash your hands!" she commanded by way of greeting, as she always did.

Jam sandwiches for tea - good. Granddad was still up

at the allotment and Mum was at work in the factory in town. Gran sat down with us at the oilcloth covered kitchen table, a cup of scalding tea in her hands. We drank milk.

Suddenly, Mitch broke the hallowed silence of teatime.

"Gran," he said, "do we have to go to school on Monday?"

Gran set her cup down with a bang and pushed her wire framed glasses further up her nose.

"Yes" she said, and picked up her cup.

We continued chewing white bread and home-made strawberry jam.

"Gran," said Mitch a second time, his mouth a sticky red mess, "when's our dad coming back?"

This time Gran put her cup down carefully and turned to face us.

"What makes you ask that?"

For once she didn't tell Mitch off for talking with his mouth full.

Mitch considered.

"Well," he said, "Johnny next-door said his dad is coming home on Monday so he won't have to go to school."

Gran folded her hands in front of her.

"Johnny's father was a prisoner of the Japanese. He nearly died. He's had to spend years in a special hospital. Thankfully he's better now and can come home but Johnny is definitely going to school. He'll see his father afterwards. That's all you need to know."

Her mouth tightened into the expression we knew meant no more talking 'or else'.

We knew nothing about our father. He'd never been around. We'd always lived with Gran and Granddad and our Mum. Mum had told us we'd been born in London eleven years earlier in the middle of an air raid. Mum said she couldn't hear if we'd cried or not for the screams and ear shattering noise of the bombs falling all around the hospital. One midwife stayed with her and they took turns at shrieking and even swearing at the tops of their voices. That's how we got our names, Mum said - after the midwife, Nurse Josephine Mitchell. We didn't believe her.

We had a mystery in our lives - our father - and it was thrilling. Nobody but Mum knew anything about him, not even Gran and Granddad, so we knew he must have been a war hero, probably a spy. All Mum would tell us was that he had had to go away to another country - even more thrilling. We decided that he was an American, just like the ones we saw in the films. Gran was tight lipped but that was natural for her and Granddad went very red if we so much as mentioned our father. Mum told us not to bother them with questions; it just made them sad. She wouldn't explain further. She wore a wedding ring but there were no wedding photographs and she was called Mrs. Sutton, the same as Gran. We are Suttons too; Mitch and Josie, the Sutton twins. It was, of course, all part of the plot to keep our father's identity safe from the Germans. The war had been over for years and to be honest we were too young when it was going on to remember much about it. Hitler was dead, we knew that, but who knew when another war would start and our father would need to become a spy again?

Johnny next-door wouldn't believe us. He said if our father was such a good spy, how come his father was captured by the Japanese and kept in a dreadful prison? He just wouldn't understand that our father was spying in Germany so how could he know about Japan? Maybe now that his father was coming home he would explain it all to him. Sometimes he can be very slow on the uptake, can Johnny. He can't read at all well and he's not particularly good at sums either. Miss Hicks, our teacher, says he's dim. She thinks he and I should both be in a special school.

That's why I like Johnny. We are alike in that we're different from the other children in our class. I can read and do sums all right. But there's one thing I can't do. I can't speak. I don't mean I'm not allowed to speak; I really can't. I can't utter a sound. When I was little I overheard Granddad telling Mum I was doing it on purpose to get attention but that's rubbish. I'd love to be able to speak. It's awful not to be able to join in conversations or put up my hand to answer questions at school, especially when I nearly always know the correct answer. I think I must have seen every doctor in the country until one doctor in London discovered that unfortunately I had been born without vocal cords. I will never be able to speak or laugh or cry out loud. I can make one noise, but Gran says that's disgusting.

A nasty old woman with whiskers on her chin tried to teach me sign language but I pretended not to be able to do it. What would be the point unless she taught everyone else in the village what the signs meant too? Anyway, I have Mitch. Maybe it's because we're twins but we seem to be able to speak to each other without actually talking.

I only have to nod or smile or even lick my lips and Mitch knows what I'm thinking and our friends know our signs too. We have our own. I didn't need old hairy chin to teach me anything, although Mum says I will have to learn eventually because I will need to communicate when I'm older and may want to do things on my own. I don't think so. Mitch and I will always be together. Johnny wouldn't believe we're twins when we were younger because Mitch and I don't look alike. I'm taller but Mitch is much stronger. He always wins arm wrestling matches. I suppose it's because I have the same colouring as Mum - brown hair, brown eyes - but Mitch is really blonde with pale blue eyes. Gran says it happens. She once knew twins who each had one brown eye and one blue.

We tried our best to stay awake that night to prolong the holiday as much as we could but inevitably the time came to go back to school. Nobody liked our teacher, Miss Hicks. She was old and crabby and shouted and threw things at us, especially at Johnny. Thank goodness this is our last year. Our village school is small so two years are taught together in one classroom by the same teacher. We had endured Horrendous Hicks for one year already. Another three terms appealed about as much as a prisoner of war camp.

As usual we dawdled down the lane, collecting schoolmates on the way, and reached the old brick school just as the bell rang and lines of children were moving towards the classrooms. In we charged, not because we were delighted to be back but in order to claim our own desks quickly, in case some newly promoted pupil or even a strange, new child sat in our place. There was no unknown child, there rarely was, but there was someone strange and new. Miss Hicks didn't bawl at us to slow down as she usually did. Miss Hicks wasn't there. Instead, beside the unlit stove stood the headmaster, Mr. Philpot, and another man. This man was shorter and slimmer than Mr. Philpot and dressed in what Granddad would call a sharp suit. He had a blue and silver striped tie and a gold ring on the little finger of his left hand. His face was pale, his mouth wide with rather thick lips but his eyes were hidden behind horn-rimmed glasses. He also had very fair hair, like Mitch.

"It's a Jerry!" hissed Johnny, but then anyone with fair hair except Mitch was a Jerry, that is a German, in

Johnny's eyes.

Mr. Philpot harrumphed and lowered his bushy eyebrows. We were quiet at once.

"Good morning class."

"Good morning, Mr. Philpot," we chorused in a deliberately sing-song rhythm and waited for him to say who the stranger was. It seemed too early in the term for a school inspector but you never knew. Mr. Philpot, solid, familiar, dressed in his usual leather patched tweed jacket and baggy grey trousers looked old and shabby beside this clean-cut stranger.

"Class," Mr. Philpot began, "I have important news for you. Sadly, Miss Hicks has had to leave us suddenly in order to look after her sick father."

Johnny began to cheer until Mitch kicked him on the ankle. Mr. Philpot ignored them and continued.

"I'm sure you will all miss her," he said pointedly, "but I'm pleased to be able to tell you that at very short notice our education department has been able to find us a substitute teacher" (here he inclined his head towards the stranger) "all the way from the United States of America."

There was an audible murmuring and twenty hands shot up in unison. There were twenty-one in our class, but it was obviously no use in me holding up my hand.

Mr. Philpot waved them down and said, "Wait until I've finished."

The new teacher had still not uttered a word. Mitch and I exchanged a meaningful glance. American - blonde hair - not a great speaker, then ... could it possibly be? I could see Mitch's eyes bright with excitement. Had our father returned?

"So, children, may I introduce your new teacher, Mr … Mitchell."

Our village is not one of those you see on calendars and greetings cards with a duck pond and thatched cottages.

In fact it is long and straggly; no pretty village green with maypole dancing in the spring and cricket teas in the summer. There is one main road where the village is set at an equal distance between two towns, Dourwell and Ashwood, with various lanes and byways off. Last year we did a local history project in school and discovered practically nothing about it. There is one pub which was probably built on the site of an old inn so it is thought the village grew up around this inn which was possibly a staging post on the way from London to Dover. It didn't even suffer much during the war. There was only one bomb that fell over the village: a doodlebug which landed in the middle of a field and caused no damage apart from a few windows that blew in from the effects of the blast. The only casualties were the farmer's cabbages.

The school is ten minutes walk down Church Lane and, as you might expect, is very near the church. There is nothing picturesque about the school. It is a plain, red brick building with playgrounds on three sides (one with outside toilets that freeze over in winter) and a small grass-and-mud field on the other. It is really just one big room, divided into three small classrooms by folding doors. Our room is slightly the larger with small windows set high in the walls, letting in howling draughts in the winter and keeping out cooling breezes in the summer. The teacher's long desk is at the far end in front of the blackboard and to one side of the old stove. Our desks, metal framed and ink stained, are crammed into the rest of the space. There are three pictures on the walls: a map of Great Britain, a painting of a vase of yellow flowers and, over the blackboard, a photograph of King George and his wife, Queen Elizabeth, even though the poor king had died and we were to have a new queen. Mitch sits with the boys on the left-hand side of the room and I sit with the girls on the other. Mitch is the only one in the school with really blonde hair although several children have what Gran calls dark blonde hair. Johnny says that's okay because the Saxons had dark blonde hair but I think he's making that up.

The new American teacher didn't teach us that first day of term; Mr. Philpot did. He said Mr. Mitchell needed to 'acclimatise'. Nobody knew what that meant so Mr. Philpot made us look it up in our dictionaries. It means 'accustom to new climate or environment'. We weren't any the wiser.

As we walked home from school, Mitch said, "I suppose that new teacher is real. I wasn't dreaming, was I?"

I shook my head.

Johnny said, "I wonder why he's come here? I shouldn't think anyone in America has heard of this village."

I could see that Mitch was dying to confide our suspicions to him, but I gave him a look. I thought we needed to find out more about this Mr. Mitchell first. After all, Mitchell is a very common surname in England, so it probably is in America too and all Mitchells there might have blonde hair. As it happened, for once Mum was in when we got home. Some machinery had broken down at the factory so all the workers had been sent home early. She was looking glum because that meant she wouldn't earn so much that week. She was certainly in no mood to be quizzed about our missing father and neither was Gran. She was always surly on wash days. They didn't even listen when Mitch told them about the new teacher, just made 'uh-huh' noises.

We were allowed out after tea for an hour. The cottages up our lane belong to Foxhole Farm. Granddad had worked there all his life until he'd had an accident on the tractor. It had turned over into a ditch and his arm had been crushed. He hasn't been able to use it since. Perhaps that's why he's always so grumpy, although Gran says he should be grateful that the farmer has let us stay on in the cottage even though he had to employ someone else to take Granddad's place. Granddad just does odd jobs around the farm now and spends a lot of time up at the allotments.

We had a meeting place in the small wood behind the hiding tree. No adult ever went there. It was unproductive, Granddad said, just a hidey hole for foxes and badgers - and children. If you looked hard enough there was a way in, curtained off by overgrown brambles and nettles as high as your head. If you were clever enough to dodge the scratches and stings and pushed your way through unwelcoming undergrowth, you came to a sort of clearing beneath a beech tree. It was here we'd made our den. We'd built it out of bits and pieces we'd found lying around or else had managed to drag in to the wood. Two large pieces of curved corrugated iron which had come from a demolished bomb shelter rested against the lower trunk of the beech. Johnny had slashed the trunk with his penknife so that the iron stayed put when we put rubble against it. Then we'd covered it with old rags we'd found and finally with branches and creeper. We even had a bit of carpet inside to sit on. We were really proud of it and only our very close friends were ever invited in.

That afternoon Cora Murphy was there. She's alright, and Mitch really likes her. She has black hair in two thick plaits and the brightest blue eyes I've ever seen. Her father also has bright blue eyes. He's from Ireland and speaks very strangely so that it is sometimes hard to understand what he's saying, but her mother is a Londoner and calls everyone 'luv'. The trouble with Cora is that she's too fussy. She's always brushing things off her dress and fiddling with her plaits which are tied with white ribbons, not the regulation school colour of navy, but somehow she gets away with it. My hair, like most of the girls in our class, is cut short with a no-nonsense straight fringe. The other thing about Cora is that her chest has started to grow. Gran says she's a forward little hussy. Of course, Johnny should have been there but he was busy meeting with his father.

We sat in the den (Cora knelt down because she didn't want to soil her dress) and talked about the new teacher. I always carry a notebook and a pencil so I can write down things that are too long or complicated to have signs for.

"Fancy Mr. Mitchell coming all this way," Cora said, "do you think he'll be better than Horrendous?"

"Of course he will," Mitch said stoutly, "He's American, so he's sure to be friendly. All Americans are friendly; Mum says they gave ladies nylon stockings in the war. Perhaps he'll give us chewing gum!"

"Do you think we'll understand what he says?" I wrote.

"I will," said Cora.

"Well, you're used to funny voices."

Cora flared up. "What do you mean by that?"

I could see Mitch winding himself up to be the peacemaker when our attention was caught by the sound of the undergrowth being slashed back. We fell quiet. We were worried that it might be Stinky Jim, an old tramp who often came to our village knocking on back doors asking for a bite to eat or any old clothes. We weren't scared of him, everyone knew he wasn't quite right in the head but completely harmless. Every Christmas he would break a window in the telephone box on the main road while the village policeman, Constable Banks, looked the other way. Then he would arrest Stinky so that he could spend Christmas in a warm police cell and be given a Christmas dinner. However, he wasn't called Stinky for nothing so we didn't want him to discover our private place.

Mitch crawled silently to the mouth of the den and looked out. It wasn't Stinky Jim; it was Johnny. We were very surprised to see him for two reasons: we were not expecting him and he knew better than to make a path to our den. He had a thick stick in his hand with which he was striking out at the brambles and nettles. Mitch hissed at him to stop. Johnny still hadn't looked at us. He was staring at his feet and saying nothing. Mitch stood up and took the stick out of his unresisting hand.

"What are you doing? Why aren't you at home?"

Johnny wouldn't meet Mitch's eye. He turned his head sideways and mumbled something.

Cora said, "Are you in trouble?"

A huge sigh escaped from Johnny and he sort of crumpled where he was, sitting on a bramble that he hardly seemed to notice. I went over to him and put my arm around his shoulders. Something was very wrong.

It seemed to take Johnny several minutes before he could explain. It appeared that his father had come home from the hospital while we were in school and Johnny had rushed in to see him but then had had a shock. The man sitting in the kitchen was not his father. Of course his mother and his aunt who lived with them said it was. The man even went to give him a hug but Johnny shrunk away. His mother had warned him before he went off to school that morning that his father would look different to the man in the photograph. Johnny was only two years old when his father was captured by the Japanese and they'd only met once, when Johnny was a small baby, so he only knew what his father looked like from the photograph his mother kept on her bedside table. However, Johnny said the man in the kitchen wasn't one little bit like the man in the photo. That father was handsome and smiling, tall and well built with lots of dark hair, like Johnny really. The man who claimed to be his father was very thin, his hair was scant and grey, his skin scarred and anyway, he looked much too old.

Suddenly Johnny became very angry. His mother had gone to visit his father in hospital hundreds of times since the end of the war, and his aunt, who was his father's unmarried sister, had gone too but Johnny was never allowed to go. So he had a theory. He said he realised now that his real father had died and that his mother and aunt had conspired to give a home to some old patient who had nowhere to go and so that people wouldn't talk behind their backs were trying to pass off this man as his father. He started to cry. We were really shocked. Johnny never cried, not even when Horrendous Hicks threw a wooden backed board rubber that had hit him on the head.

I tightened my hold on his shoulders and Cora patted his hand.

"I don't think that can be right," she said. "His ration book would be in another name for a start."

She was right. There was still a shortage of some things because of the war which meant everyone had to share what there was so we had coupons that could be exchanged at the shops for food like meat and for sweets.

Johnny's head lifted a bit until Mitch said, "Maybe he doesn't eat meat or like sweets so he doesn't need a ration book."

Sometimes my brother can be so unhelpful.

"What?" he said, at the look both Cora and I gave him.

In the end, we agreed to make a pact to help Johnny find out if the man was his father or not. It was too soon to make a pact about our own suspicions that the new teacher was our father. That would come later.

Over night, it seemed, school became the one place where we wanted to be. Mum and Gran smiled at our

12

eagerness but Granddad, as usual, tried to put us off by saying that Americans weren't to be trusted. It was something to do with them being late for the war. Mr. Mitchell's accent was not quite as strong as we'd imagined it would be. He said we'd been watching too many cowboy films. However, it was strange enough to make all he said fascinating. He had different words for things like trousers (he called them pants!) and the board rubber which he called an eraser. There were others too and we had to teach him the correct words. It was fun! He was very interested in Mitch and me. The others thought it was because we were twins and Mitch had the same name as him but we knew that was only part of the truth. He never talked to us about our relationship or asked us to keep it a secret but we did. We sort of hugged the knowledge to us and the waiting time before it became known, before Mr. Mitchell finally met up with our Mum, had us almost dancing with excitement.

Chapter 2

Our Mum is lovely in all ways. Her hair is normally straight but her friend Mavis perms it for her so that her curls bounce when she walks. She is normal height too but she has a long neck which somehow makes her look taller. Her eyes are brown with long eye lashes but she doesn't wear glasses like Gran. She is really kind and never shouts at us. The best thing about her is her voice. She can sing, our Mum. She sings all the latest songs and I mime the words and we pretend to be on the wireless. She used to go to dances now and then with Mavis but now she says she's too old for such things. However she's only seventeen years older than us so I'm not sure about that. I think she stopped going out with Mavis because Granddad didn't like it. He was always saying she'd only get into trouble again. I didn't know what he meant, but it made Mum look very sad.

Sometimes, when she thought we weren't watching her, she had that sad look and sometimes even sighed. We didn't like that. We thought it was because she had had a brother, Uncle Peter, who was killed in the war just before we were born. She has a photo of him on her bedside table, just like Johnny's Mum has one of his father. There's another one of Uncle Peter on the sideboard in the front room but we don't go in there much. Mum has to work very hard in the factory in Ashwood so we can eat and have clothes to wear. During the war the factory made parts for aircraft but now it makes irons and toasters. She would really have liked to work in an office but she hadn't learned enough shorthand at the college by the time she had us. She said we were lovely babies and she would never have given us up. I'm not sure what she meant by that but Mitch and I were excited that maybe our father had come back. Perhaps he would take us all back to America and Mum wouldn't have to work at all. It's a well-known fact that everyone in America is rich.

As I said, Mr. Mitchell was very interested in us, me in particular. I had to put up with Cora and the other girls calling me teacher's pet but I didn't care. He was very patient with me, asking me questions about my 'condition' and then waiting while I wrote the answers down. He was also patient with Johnny. Johnny had started to behave badly in school, running down the corridors and shouting and pushing the other boys. He even punched Keith and had to stay in for the next three playtimes, even though Keith had been saying that Johnny's father was an old man. Mr. Mitchell talked quietly to him until Johnny told him about his father dying in Japan. Mr. Mitchell said he'd had a friend who was killed by the Japanese in the bombing at Pearl Harbour so he knew how Johnny was feeling. Johnny said he hated the Germans as well and Mr. Mitchell smiled and said, "I guess so."

That's the thing about not being able to make a sound. A lot of the time grown-ups forget I am there. Mitch says I'd make an excellent spy and in a funny way I became one. I didn't do it deliberately, that would have been sneaky, but one day I stayed behind after the bell rang for home time. I was flower monitor that term and had forgotten to top up the water in the vases at break time as I usually did. I signed to Mitch and the others to leave without me and I'd catch them up. I went to the drinking fountain in the playground and used a milk bottle to carry the water to the classroom but when I got back Mr. Philpot was there, talking to Mr. Mitchell. I stopped in the doorway but they didn't notice me. Mr. Philpot had a letter in his hand which he was showing to Mr. Mitchell.

"I've had this communication from the Department." Mr. Philpot was saying, "Apparently they're having a problem with your references. Any idea why?"

"In what way?" Mr. Mitchell asked, frowning.

"They've had no replies. They're asking if they have the correct addresses."

Mr. Mitchell studied the letter. "Why, yes. Have they tried telephoning?"

"I really couldn't say. Did you give them the numbers?"

Mr. Mitchell pursed his lips. "Can't say I recall, but it's possible I didn't. After all, I've been away from the States for some time - can't say I exactly recall the numbers. They should be able to find them in a directory, though."

"Yes, of course. I'll suggest that."

Mr. Philpot turned to leave, and saw me. "Oh, hello, Josie, not gone home yet?" I showed him the milk bottle and pointed to the flowers.

"I see, the flowers need watering. Well, don't be too long. Your Gran will wonder where you are."

He nodded to Mr. Mitchell and left. Mr. Mitchell said nothing to me but I could feel his gaze on my back as I emptied the water into the vases. He packed some books and papers into his briefcase and held the door open for me so that I had to go quickly.

"Good-bye, Josie," he said.

Mitch got excited again when I told him about the overheard conversation.

"Don't you see," he said, "that proves Mr. Mitchell was in Germany if he hasn't been in America for years."

I was a little doubtful myself, he could have been

16

anywhere, but I didn't tell Mitch that. To be honest, I wasn't sure that I wanted Mr. Mitchell to be our father. He'd given us no sign and there had been plenty of times when he could have had a private conversation with us and asked after our mother. Why would he keep away from her if he loved her? If he didn't, then he wouldn't love us either. That would be unbearable after waiting all these years.

Sometimes when I tried to explain to Gran how I felt, how lost I was not knowing who my father was and how there was a great longing in my heart she would either brush me off saying, "Isn't this family enough for you, then?" or give a bitter laugh and say "You're only eleven years old - you don't understand these things." But it was Gran who didn't understand.

Sometimes I looked in the mirror and hardly recognised myself. It wasn't that my face and body were changing like Cora's, but all the same I was growing away from the little girl I used to be. Perhaps my body wasn't ready to grow up just yet but my mind was. I had deep thoughts about things - the war, my family, the future - and it was scary. I know what I want to do in the future. I love words; the look of them, the sound of them. I can't say them aloud so I practice saying them in my head. I can have long conversations with myself or sometimes with people who only exist in my mind. It helps me feel normal. I know what I want to do. I want to write books; I just don't know how to go about it. I wanted to talk to Mum about all this but she had enough worries and Mitch and I had a pact not to add to them. All the same, I was upset that Gran didn't or couldn't understand how I was feeling.

One day, just before the half-term holiday, Mr. Mitchell asked the class what we were doing for Halloween. We had to admit we didn't know what he was talking about. He looked shocked.

"You must know about Halloween," he said, "you know, spooks an' all? Dressing up as ghosts and zombies and going out Trick or Treating?"

"No" we chorused.

"Y'mean, English children don't do this?"

The afternoon's lesson was forgotten as Mr. Mitchell told us all about Halloween and how the children in America had a high old time with dressing up, parties and presents.

"Can't do that," said Mitch, ever the practical one. "There's no money to spare for parties or presents."

Mr. Mitchell considered for a moment, then he said, "Then we'll have our own Halloween party the last day of half-term. Anyone got an apple tree in their yard?"

Several hands shot up and Mr. Mitchell soon had it organised that those who could do so would bring in any stored apples their families could spare. He commandeered a large bucket from the caretaker and explained about bobbing for apples. This meant trying to pick up apples from a bucket of water with only our teeth. Then he suggested we asked our mothers for any white cloth, such as old sheets, that they might be able to let us have so that we could make ghost costumes. He also asked if we grew pumpkins.

Looking at our blank faces, he said "I guess not."

Then he told us what pumpkins were, and how they were hollowed out and faces cut into them. Graham Parker had a great idea.

"Could we use big swedes instead?" he asked.

Mr. Mitchell's face was a picture until we explained that Graham was talking about vegetables, not people from Sweden! There was such an excited buzz of chatter that Mr. Philpot came in to see what was going on.

When it was explained to him, he said, "I see. Not

too keen on the idea of celebrating ghosts and suchlike myself."

There was a loud groan, and he held up his hand, palm outwards.

"However, as it will help you understand the customs of another country, you may go ahead."

The groans were replaced by loud cheers. Mr. Mitchell was smiling broadly but Mr. Philpot just nodded to him and left.

I think the phrase for our families' faces when we told them about Halloween is 'somewhat bemused' but they rallied round. I heard Cora's mother say it was about time the children enjoyed themselves, whatever it was all about. We had a great time. Some children dressed up as ghosts in white sheets and all of us used chalk to make our faces white and smeared coal dust around our eyes. We did look ghoulish! It was a shame it all came off in the water when we played ducking for apples.

Johnny and Mitch had found a really big swede, one of the cream coloured ones, and had made a superb Halloween lantern. It had been really hard to hollow it out even a little bit but Johnny had managed to do it and to cut slits for the eyes and the mouth. We'd found a stub of candle which we fixed inside. When we lit it, the lantern looked really frightening. It was far too good to throw away after school but Mitch had an idea. We would find a big strong stick, tie the lantern on the end and then swing it by our back door to frighten Gran. She was a good sport really and would laugh a lot after her fright.

It was dusk when we left school, later than usual because the party overran. We left Cora at her door but Mitch and Johnny and I were in high spirits after the fun we'd had and the prospect of 'frightening' Gran. We couldn't run in case the candle in the lantern went out so it was beginning to get dark when we reached home. Johnny came too because Gran had invited his mum and aunt and the man she said was his dad for tea. As we got near the kitchen door, I motioned for the boys to stop.

"If we go to the door they'll see us and the surprise will be spoilt." I wrote, "Let's creep up the side of the house and wave the lantern up at the window."

"Great idea" the boys agreed, so we did just that.

We crouched low under the uncurtained window and Johnny, as the tallest, held the stick with the lantern up to the window and made whoo-ing noises. Mitch could hardly stop himself from laughing out loud. We had expected the grown-ups to perhaps gasp or even yell a bit but we certainly did not expect the reaction we actually got. We had never heard screams like it - and they didn't come from the women. We found out afterwards that Gran and Johnny's mum and aunt were sitting at the table with their backs to the window but Granddad and the man known as Mr. Gibbs were sitting directly opposite. When Johnny swung our lantern across the window Mr. Gibbs went deathly pale, sprang to his feet upsetting the tea things and started to scream, his arms across his face.

We didn't wait for the screaming to stop. We ran as fast as we could back to school, the only safe place we could think of. It was getting quite dark and there are no street lights in the village. Johnny had dropped the Halloween lantern when Mr. Gibbs screamed and the candle flame had gone out. We ran down our lane and then down Church Lane to the school without stopping. We saw no-one, not even a dog. Thankfully, when we reached the school there was a light on and we hammered on the door, Mitch and Johnny crying out to be let in. We heard running footsteps and Mr. Philpot flung the door wide.

"What on earth …" he began, but Mitch and Johnny began talking at once and didn't make any sense. Mr. Philpot ushered us into his study where he had been working on some papers, now in disarray on his desk, and calmed us down. Soon he had the whole story out of us and at first said nothing, looking at the ceiling and thinking.

Then he said, "I'd better get you home before your families send out the search parties. Now, this is what I want you to do. You are to say how very sorry you are for playing such a silly prank. However, there is no way you could have known how much it would upset John's father so I will explain that to your families. Now, I will lock up here and we'll all ride back in my car - and John, do stop snivelling."

Even though we were dreading the reception we'd get at home, it was a great treat to ride in Mr. Philpot's car. No-one in our families owned one and I think perhaps it was the first time Johnny had been in one at all. All too soon, Mr. Philpot pulled up outside our house and opened the doors for us to get out. Granddad was standing by the gate, Mum and Gran behind him. I thought he was going to bellow at us but of course with Mr. Philpot there he had to be polite. It wasn't every day that someone as important as the headmaster called at our house and we were all shown in to the front room away from the clutter of the kitchen. Gran asked Mr. Philpot to please take a seat but we were left standing. Mr. Philpot explained how we had sought sanctuary, as he put it, in his office and then motioned to us. It was our cue to say our piece, which we did. Then Mr. Philpot asked to speak to Granddad in private so the rest of us went back in the kitchen. Mum put bread and cheese and pickle on the table and we had a very belated tea. She and Gran didn't say much but Mum smiled at us and said "Never mind, you weren't to know." Mum took Johnny home then so he could apologise to his family. Mitch and I were expecting to be sent to bed but Gran was far too intent on keeping us quiet so she could eavesdrop on the conversation in the front room. I don't know if she heard much of it but she quickly scuttled back from the connecting door when the armchairs creaked as the two men got up.

The next morning the doctor called at Johnny's house and spent a long time talking to Mr. Gibbs. Then he asked to see us. Somewhat in awe, we all three went to see him in Mrs. Gibbs's front room. He was a kindly man, Doctor Simmonds. I knew him well, of course, because he had had to authorise all the visits to the doctors in London that Mum and I had made. He smiled at us and told us to sit on the settee. Then he explained what had happened to Mr. Gibbs, who was in bed upstairs.

Johnny was very quiet and very pale as Doctor Simmonds explained that while Mr. Gibbs had been in the prisoner of war camp he and the other prisoners had been very badly treated, both physically and mentally. That meant the Japanese guards had tormented and bullied the prisoners so much that now men like Mr. Gibbs had terrible nightmares. He said that seeing our Halloween lantern with its yellow skin and slit like eyes had reminded him so much of those guards that he couldn't stop himself from screaming. Doctor Simmonds said that that didn't mean he was a coward, just the opposite. He had been a very brave man, had had to be to survive such a horrific camp, but seeing our lantern had caused his mind to relive that terrible time. He finished by saying no-one was blaming us, it was just an unfortunate incident. Then he gave Johnny a very serious look and put his hand on his shoulder.

"Johnny," he said, "he really is your father and although his hair will always be grey, with your help he will get back to the man he was before he was captured."

Johnny just nodded but I could see tears welling up in his eyes. Doctor Simmonds turned to go and then he looked

22

back, his hand on the doorknob.

"Just one more thing, all of you. Don't grow up hating Japanese people. Even your father, Johnny, acknowledges that it was just the soldiers who were so hateful. And remember - thousands of innocent Japanese civilians, a lot of them children, suffered horribly when the Americans dropped the atom bombs on them."

We were shocked into immobility. I suppose it was only seconds that we sat there completely dumbfounded before Mum and Mrs. Gibbs called us back into the kitchen but we felt as though the doctor had turned our world upside down. I had heard Granddad say, spitting with anger, that if the Americans hadn't bombed those 'slit-eyed devils' then Johnny's father would never have been rescued. Now the doctor was telling us not to hate them. Who was right? We never told the grown-ups what he had said, sensing that it would cause more trouble and probably a biting lecture from Granddad. Even so I took a long time getting to sleep that night, thinking about the doctor's plea to us. We had been taught by our families that the Japanese were an evil nation, as were the Germans, but Doctor Simmonds' words about the suffering caused by the atom bombs disturbed me greatly. Just how the victims had suffered I didn't know, but I did know about the people in England who had been killed or badly injured by bombing without they themselves being involved in the fighting. It was all part of the war, I supposed, but for the first time I thought about mothers and children in enemy countries who were killed and injured by ours or the Americans' bombs. I suppose that night I took my first step into realising that growing up did not necessarily mean growing wiser.

That night it rained heavily. We never went to the den in wet weather as the wood was hardly a welcoming place then. We made an exception the next morning though, as we had so much to think about and discuss. As we crawled through the undergrowth bramble leaves seemed to delight in dripping rainwater down our necks and the going underfoot was dangerously slippery. We had called for Cora first and had had to wait while she changed into an old windcheater and Wellington boots. Gran always says that children are a perverse lot - 'you never know how they will react to anything'. I think she's wrong; it's adults who are unpredictable. Just think what happened when we found the body!

Chapter 3

We had pushed our way through dripping branches and brambles and sighed with relief to reach the beech clearing. Our den, of course, would be soaking wet so it was no good going inside but this was our private place where we could talk away from prying adults. Johnny saw the body first. It was a man, lying on his back just outside the entrance to our den. He was soaking wet and covered in mud. His eyes were shut and close to one hand was a broken bottle. We crept nearer until we all recognised Stinky Jim.

"Oh, no," said Cora, wrinkling her nose, "do you think he's been in our den?"

Mitch shook his head."Don't know. What d'you think he died of?"

Never having seen a dead body before, we were very curious. Squatting down, we studied Stinky Jim. He was filthy but that was his natural state. However, he was without his usual flat cap and we were intrigued to see that he was bald even though he had a huge, matted grey beard.

I wrote, "Do you think we should try to move him?"

"Yes!" Cora said, "get him away from our den before anyone comes and finds it."

"Who's going to come?" Johnny asked, "I don't suppose anyone is looking for him."

All the same we decided it would be a good idea to move Stinky Jim further into the bushes - after all, bodies are found there all the time in films - so the boys took a boot each and started to heave. Suddenly there was a sound like a cow bellowing for her calf, and it came from the body. The boys dropped it and we all jumped back towards the den.

"Rats," Johnny swore, "I think he's still alive."

This was even worse. It meant that Stinky Jim had discovered the way into the beech clearing and it was no longer our secret. The body opened one eye and regarded us.

"Help," it said, in a hoarse voice.

"We thought you were dead," said Mitch.

Stinky Jim's eyes were full of pain."Help," he croaked again.

"Where do you hurt?" Cora, who was going to be a nurse, asked him but Stinky Jim's eyes had closed again.

We had a long discussion what to do. He might only be an old tramp but we felt proud that an adult had asked for our help. On the other hand, if we brought people here that would be the end of our secret den. Finally Cora said that if we didn't get help soon Stinky Jim would die and we might be blamed.

As it happened, the first people we saw were Granddad and Constable Banks, passing the time of day. At first they thought we were having them on, but Cora is very persuasive and eventually they came with us to the clearing. We thought they would be very calm and know precisely what to do but in fact they were a lot more shocked than we had been. Constable Banks rushed back to the police house to phone for an ambulance. We were told to go home and not get in the way, even though Stinky Jim was our find. Later that evening, after we'd been sent to bed, Mitch and I crept half-way down the stairs to listen in on the adults' conversation. It appeared that Stinky Jim had been attacked. He'd obviously been having his supper, going by the broken beer bottle by his hand, when someone had whacked him around the head with something heavy. He had a fractured skull and Gran said that, considering the

26

bad weather, he was lucky he was used to living out of doors or else he might have died from exposure. Stinky was in the hospital recovering, but had been given medicine to make him sleep and get better so he couldn't tell the police exactly what had happened or who had attacked him or why. That was the mystery; he obviously didn't have anything to steal.

Of course, our private place had been ruined. We left the den forever that morning but surprisingly it didn't upset me as much as I thought it would. Mitch felt much the same and we decided it was because we were actually too old to have a den. We had loved it but it was time to move on, although to where we couldn't quite imagine. We would be taking the eleven-plus examination soon and the results would decide which secondary school we would attend. Once that happened it would mean we were well on the way to becoming adults. It was a strange feeling, as though we couldn't wait for it to happen but it was worrying all the same. It was like the time Mum took us to the seaside and we persuaded her to let us go on the Ghost Train at the funfair. It was thrilling but I was glad Mum was with us.

The rest of the week was uneventful and on the following Sunday we went to Sunday school as usual and most of our friends went too, although not Cora as she was a Catholic. Graham Parker said we were sent to Sunday school not because we ought to learn about Jesus but because our mothers wanted us out of the way while they cooked the Sunday roast. Whatever the reason, I liked it. The vicar was very old and quite deaf but our Sunday school teacher, Mrs. Clay, was a warm and cuddly sort of lady who had no children of her own. Even so, she was very good at telling us stories. Even the boys listened without fidgeting. That morning it was the story of the Good Samaritan who had stopped to help a badly injured man.

"And," Mrs. Clay finished, "we have some Good Samaritans of our very own, don't we?"

Everybody turned to look at us. I was expecting the others to pull faces and whisper "teacher's pet" but nobody did.

Mitch said, almost carelessly, "Anybody would have helped him."

"I should hope so," said Mrs. Clay, "but it happened to be you three and Cora. Well done; but for you old Jim may well have died."

I felt a bit guilty then, remembering how we'd thought Stinky was dead and the time we took before we got help and I could see by the blush on both Mitch and Johnny's faces that they had had the same thought.

Then Graham asked the one thing that was on all our minds.

"Who do you think attacked him, Miss?"

Mrs. Clay regarded us thoughtfully. "I have no idea," she said, "but I know this. God knows and it is up to him what he does about it so don't you go playing detectives. You don't want to get yourselves into trouble."

When Sunday school was over, Mrs. Clay called the three of us to her.

"I meant what I said. I know you found Jim so it's your adventure but let it go now. Remember the Good Samaritan. He knew he couldn't take care of the injured man so he left him to someone who could."

Mitch bristled a bit on Cora's behalf as she always claimed she knew a lot of first aid, until Mrs. Clay added, "You know, the good Samaritan never tried to find out who had injured the man. Sometimes, however curious we are, we have to leave things be." She knew us well. If only we had taken her advice.

The weather was wet and windy when we returned to

school. Guy Fawkes Night was looming large and the anticipation of bonfires, fireworks and the novelty of cooking potatoes in the hot ashes, plus anxiety regarding the weather, soon overtook the mystery of Stinky Jim in our friends' minds, if not our own. There was always a huge village bonfire on the school field and most of the boys were busy after school collecting old wooden crates and fallen tree branches, plus any other bits and pieces that would burn, before assembling them into a satisfying pile in the middle of the field supervised by Mr. Philpot and Constable Banks. Because of that, it wasn't easy for the four of us to get together. Cora and I were left by ourselves to talk over the problem. Stinky Jim was conscious but couldn't tell the police anything much, only that he was hit from behind, something the doctors already knew from the position of his wound. He apparently didn't know anyone who wished him harm. Most of the village assumed it was another tramp after his bottle of beer. Cora's father said if it had been a bottle of Guinness he would have understood it.

Cora and I didn't think that could be the reason. There was the mystery of our father, the mystery of Johnny's father and now the mystery of Stinky Jim. We seemed to be the only ones in the village who still wondered about it. It seemed to us that grown-ups sometimes just want to be able to tidy away anything they don't understand so that they won't have to waste time thinking about it. Perhaps if they did they would then have to do something about it and that would upset their routine. It was obviously up to us to do their thinking for them.

One day after school while the boys were busy collecting wood, Cora asked me round to her house for tea. Mrs. Murphy had made Marmite sandwiches and orange squash for us and Cora's brothers, a real treat. They were pests, Cora's brothers. The little one who was in the Infants wasn't too bad but Kevin, who was in the class below us, was a proper sneak. He was always taking things in for Miss Napier, his teacher, so that he could be teacher's pet. We'd never let him anywhere near our den or everyone in the village would have known about it. He could never keep his mouth shut no matter what Cora threatened him with so when he started to question us about Mr. Mitchell, Cora told him to shut up. Cora's Mum didn't like that.

"Don't talk to your brother like that," she snapped, "he's only curious. Come to that, so am I. He's a bit of a rum 'un, that Mr. Mitchell, ain't he?"

Cora frowned. "What do you mean, Mum?"

"Well, now," Mrs. Murphy could never resist a good gossip, even if it was only with us, "he's a real mystery man, you must admit. He's never said where in America he comes from or anything about his family - nothing about himself at all. Kevin here says Miss Napier really fancies him, but he wouldn't go to the pictures with her when she asked him."

In spite of ourselves, we were intrigued.

"How does Kevin know that?" Cora asked then, looking at her shame-faced brother, "You were listening at keyholes again, weren't you?"

Kevin flinched, waiting for the weight of Cora's hand but her Mum broke in quickly.

"I've seen her giving him the glad eye too, but he isn't interested in a scrag end like her. I reckon he's got his eye on your Mum, Josie."

I was shocked. How did Mrs. Murphy know that?

"He's never seen her," I wrote.

Mrs. Murphy laughed. "Oh yes he has - at the bus stop. He's waiting for the bus back to Ashwood when your Mum gets off the bus after work. I've seen the smiles and looks he gives her," and she winked at me.

If I'd had a voice, I'd still have been speechless.

Perhaps Mitch was right after all, perhaps Mr. Mitchell was our father and Mum and he had been meeting in secret because Granddad doesn't like Americans. I wanted to keep these thoughts to myself but Mitch always knows when I'm trying to hide something and he soon had it out of me.

He was very excited, and kept saying "I told you so! I told you so!"

Naturally, we didn't say anything to Mum or Gran and especially not Granddad. We realised it was early days yet. Obviously they had to work out what to say to Granddad to bring him round.

I suppose I'd got used to the idea by the time Guy Fawkes Night came. The weather changed for the better just in time. It was muddy underfoot and the men were worried that the wood on the bonfire hadn't had enough time to dry out but it was a dry, sharp evening and all of us were well wrapped up in scarves, hats and gloves with thick socks and Wellington boots on our feet. We each had a potato ready to cook in the embers as the bonfire died down. Constable Banks had fixed a thick rope a few feet away from and all the way around the bonfire and we all had to stand outside it, for safety. Only he and Mr. Philpot were allowed inside. They were in charge of the bonfire and Cora's father was in charge of the fireworks. The bonfire was a magnificent pile that towered over our heads. On top of the fire, roped to a three-legged chair, was the guy the boys had made. It was as tall as a man, stuffed with straw and dressed in tatty trousers, a torn and stained coat tied in the middle with a piece of string and a ragged hat over a painted face. It was quite wonderful.

Every family arrived with a few fireworks which they handed to Mr. Murphy. He kept them in a tin box, well away from stray sparks from the fire. The bonfire couldn't be lit until the vicar came so we waited in an agony of

31

suspense until the vicarage door opened and the vicar, leaning on Mrs. Clay, finally arrived. At once Constable Banks stepped smartly inside the rope barrier, splashed a can of paraffin on the wood and standing well back, threw a lighted taper on to the bonfire. There was a general intake of breath until the first orange flames lit up the night. In the meantime, Mr. Murphy had placed the first rocket of the evening into an empty milk bottle, firmly wedged in the soft ground. He lit the blue paper and the rocket soared upwards, scattering bright stars and flashes in its wake. We all cheered. Flames took hold of the bonfire, rocket followed rocket, Roman candles and pretty fountains poured out sparkling gold and silver droplets and there were plenty of bangers to make the boys cheer and the girls shriek. Catherine wheels were pinned to the nearest tree and with a helpful poke from a stick were made to spin in a dizzying round of rainbow colours. It was a grand display.

We weren't expecting our teachers, save for Mr. Philpot, to be there but all three were - Miss Blake, Miss Napier and of course Mr. Mitchell. They must have stayed on after school had finished. I was standing close to Mum, both of us warming ourselves by the heat of the fire from where I could see Miss Napier talking animatedly to Mr. Mitchell. He suddenly caught my eye and, smiling, excused himself and walked over to us. Miss Napier looked as though she'd sucked a lemon.

"That's a great fire," he said. "Miss Napier's been telling me all about the Gunpowder Plot, how Guy Fawkes tried to blow up the Government. I was a bit concerned that burning a man, even in effigy, would be a bit frightening for children but the horrors seem to be enjoying it."

Mum smiled. "They've been brought up with it. They all know their history and they know the guy isn't real. After all, they made it."

"I guess so," he replied, "but it gives me a weird

feeling all the same and your guy kinda reminds me of someone."

I pulled at Mum's coat to get her attention, and held my nose. She laughed, knowing who I meant.

"Yes," she replied, "I suppose it does look a little like Stinky Jim."

Mr. Mitchell looked at her sharply but just then Constable Banks, who was tending the fire, gave a loud shout.

"Ware over there!" he shouted, making shooing gestures with his arms. The bonfire hadn't been quite as well constructed as had been thought and now it was burning more fiercely on one side than the other. As Constable Banks shouted the chair holding the guy slipped sideways, a large branch was displaced and the guy turned a half-somersault ending head down on a level with Mr. Mitchell's face. His reaction took us by surprise. He leapt backwards and sort of spat out a loud exclamation. I presumed it was a swear word but I couldn't be certain because it was in another language and I was almost sure that that language was German.

I think I was subdued for the rest of the evening. I did all the usual things, cooked my potato, fooled about with my friends and wrote my name with a sparkler held in my gloved hand but I couldn't help thinking of Mr. Mitchell and the German word he'd cried out. Finally, all the fireworks had been set off and the bonfire had died down. Guided by the light of torches and lanterns we began to disperse to our own homes. Mum came to round up Mitch and me. Mr. Mitchell was with her. They were talking about Stinky Jim.

"Oh yes," Mum was saying, "he's out of hospital now and being cared for in the convalescent home in Ramsgate. Constable Banks went to see him and he says Stinky is giving the staff a right old time."

She turned to Mitch. "You know what he's always saying, Mitch?"

"I do," said Mitch, grinning, "I bet he's telling them 'I knows all about you. I'll tell the authorities about you, I will!'"

Mum laughed but I noticed Mr. Mitchell give a start.

"Why would he say that?" he asked.

"He always says that to people he hasn't met before," she replied. "He was wounded in the first war and it's addled his brains, poor chap."

"I see" said Mr. Mitchell, but he looked as if he didn't.

He was becoming more of a mystery, to me, anyway. What did it mean? I know Mum had heard the German word too but she didn't mention it to me. It was confusing but before I went to sleep that night a solution came to me. If Mitch was right and Mr. Mitchell had spent the war spying in Germany, then he must know the language. Perhaps seeing the guy fall had brought back a bad memory for him, just like with Johnny's father and the Halloween lantern. Yes, I convinced myself that would be it.

Chapter 4

The next day, we had to go to school as usual. Walking there, the others were chatting and joking about the fireworks but I was thinking about Mr. Mitchell.

Johnny came and walked next to me.

"Are you all right, Josie?" he asked, "You look down in the dumps."

I gave him a weak smile and signalled that I was fine.

Johnny wasn't fooled. "Well, if you don't want to tell me …" he shrugged.

I was slightly shocked that Johnny had noticed that I wasn't quite myself and yet Mitch hadn't. He was walking with Cora and laughing at her jokes.

School time passed as normal that week. Mr. Mitchell made no comment about Guy Fawkes Night even though several of our friends asked him if he'd enjoyed it. He just said it was very good and left it at that.

That Friday evening as all the family were listening to the wireless Mum, looking nervous, cleared her throat loudly. Gran looked at her quizzically but said nothing.

In the end Mum said to no-one in particular "There's a dance over in Ashwood tomorrow night."

Granddad looked up from his newspaper.

"So?" he said.

Mum wouldn't look at him.

"I've been asked if I'd like to go."

"What, with that Mavis?" Granddad said. "Thought you'd decided you were too old for dances."

"Not by Mavis." Mum gave us a quick look. "I've

35

been asked to go by Mr. Mitchell."

Apart for the music from the wireless, there was silence. Granddad reached over and switched it off.

"I presume you turned him down." he said.

Mum looked at him then, a sort of fire in her eyes.

"I'm going" she said simply.

Granddad started to go red and we held our breath.

Gran said, "Well, at least we'll know who she'll be with," and gave Granddad one of her looks. "What will you wear, love?"

It was settled. Granddad took himself off to his shed at the bottom of the garden and Mum and Gran went to search through Mum's wardrobe. Mitch and I looked at one another in wonder. Was this it? The big reveal? Would Mr. Mitchell now own up to being our father? Mitch was grinning wide enough to split his face in two but although I thought I was pleased one part of me was still apprehensive and the feeling would not go away.

Mr. Mitchell wasn't going to call for Mum, they would meet up outside the dance hall. Mavis came round in the morning to set Mum's hair and discuss how jealous Miss Napier would be and Gran ironed her best blue dress for her. After dinner Granddad disappeared to the allotment, taking a grumbling Mitch with him to help. I thought about going next door to confess all to Johnny but he had gone to a football match with his now acknowledged father. Mrs. Gibbs called it their getting-to-know-each-other time.

Granddad and Mitch came home in time for tea and then went down to the shed where Granddad was helping Mitch to make a champion bodge cart. The bus to Ashwood left at half-past seven. Mum would have to get a taxi back. I hoped Mr. Mitchell would pay for it. Although it was dark, Gran and I went to the gate to wave her off.

Then Gran said, "I'm just popping next door for half-an-hour. You'll be alright Josie, won't you? Granddad and

Mitch are in the shed."

I nodded and went back indoors, feeling miserable and lonely. Everyone seemed to have somebody to talk to except me. The other girls at school are friendly but they chatter a lot and forget I can't join in. Apart from Cora, no-one has the patience to wait until I can write down what I want to say.

I went upstairs to the bedroom and lay on my bed, trying to read, but I couldn't settle. I really couldn't understand why I should be so apprehensive about Mum going out with Mr. Mitchell who, after all, was probably our father, but I was. Suddenly I missed Mum terribly. I got up and pushed open the door of her bedroom. I flung myself on her bed, burying my face in her pillow. I didn't want to share her with our teacher, father or not. With a silent sob I turned over, inadvertently flinging out my arm and catching the photograph of Uncle Peter on her bedside table. It was sent crashing to the floor, glass side down. I froze in horror, knowing how much the photo meant to her. Gingerly I picked it up by the cardboard strut on the back and the whole thing came apart. To my surprise I saw another, smaller photograph tucked between Uncle Peter's photo and the backing card. I picked it up. It was a studio photograph of a young man with the words "All my love, Peter" written in one corner. I studied it, confused, for the man in the photo bore no resemblance to the large photo of Uncle Peter. I could see even from a black and white print that this Peter had light hair and a completely different shaped face. It was squarer and the smiling mouth was much wider. He reminded me of someone but I couldn't think who. Who was he, why had he signed himself as Peter and why had Mum hidden his photo behind that of her brother?

Thankfully, the glass front was tough and had not been damaged. I had a bit of a job reassembling the whole frame and getting the strange photo back in exactly the right spot but I managed it in the end and put it back on the bedside table. Guiltily, I plumped up the pillow and straightened the bedding and went back downstairs. Gran was just coming in the kitchen door.

"Are those two still in the shed?" she asked. "Take the torch Josie and go and tell them it's time you and Mitch were getting ready for bed."

Mitch and I had beds in the same room, opposite each other. That night neither of us could sleep, Mitch presumably because he was excited at Mum going out with Mr. Mitchell and I because I had even deeper worries now. I lay there trying to decide whether to tell Mitch about the photo or keep it to myself. I just couldn't make up my mind.

Breakfast the next morning was a stilted affair. Normally, because we don't need to set off for Sunday school until ten o'clock we take our time over the meal, talking and signing to each other and enjoying the one cooked breakfast of the week. However, it soon became apparent that Granddad was refusing to talk to Mum except for such things as "pass the salt". Neither did Gran refer to Mum's date with Mr. Mitchell. Mum herself was quiet. I'd expected her to be different somehow, to perhaps be smiley and happy but she showed no signs of being particularly excited.

It was a relief to escape to Sunday school with Mitch and Johnny and the others. Cora, being a Catholic, went to the big church in Ashwood with her family so I didn't have her to confide in but I'd thought of someone else who would be sympathetic. Mrs. Clay. There was no opportunity to talk to her in private so I decided to write her a letter.

I knew where she lived, of course. Everyone knows each other in this small village. She lived on her own as her husband had died before she moved here five years ago but she had made lots of friends and was well liked. She did cleaning for the vicar and Doctor Simmonds and his wife but she never gossiped about them. I think some of the ladies in the village were a bit annoyed by that. I took a long time thinking what to write. Would she think I was gossiping or worse, spying on people? How much could I tell her without breaking the pact Mitch and I had agreed on? It was very difficult. In the end, this is what I wrote:

Dear Mrs Clay,
I hope you don't mind me writing to you but as you know I can't actually talk to you but I need to discuss things with someone and I can't talk to Mum because some of it concerns her and I can't talk to Gran because she thinks I shouldn't have worries at my age. I have had bad dreams about my life such as what will happen to me when I have to go to the secondary school and I won't have any friends because I won't be able to join in their chat and how will I make the teachers understand me. I don't want to go to a special school because I would have to board and leave Mitch and Mum and everyone and that would make me awfully sad. Also Mum has been to the dance with Mr. Mitchell and I'm worried because he said a German word.
Yours faithfully,
Josephine Sutton xx

I found an old envelope in the waste bin and put my letter in it. It had Granddad's name - Mr. W. Sutton - and our address on the front so I scratched all that out and wrote Mrs. Clay's name on it instead. It took an awful lot of courage to post the letter in her front door. Twice I walked up her garden path and twice I ran back. Finally, I ran up the path, shoved the envelope through her letter box and ran away quickly. I knew I was putting a lot of trust in her but I was so desperate to tell somebody my troubles that

that overcame my fears.

Now that we didn't have a den to meet in the four of us took to going for walks around the village whenever we had something private to discuss. Mitch and I had had a long conversation regarding Mr. Mitchell. We'd decided that now Mum was going out with him it wouldn't be long before people would know that he was our father. It would be unkind of us not to tell our best friends before everyone else knew. With that in mind, we'd called for Johnny one day after school and then for Cora. Her house was at the far end of the lane so we began to walk back the way we had come. It took Mitch some courage to raise the matter of our father but in the end he did so.

Johnny was flabbergasted and kept saying things like "He can't be, he's American!" but Cora was more thoughtful.

"Well," she said in the grown-up voice she uses to talk to her brothers, "I suppose it's a possibility but I think we need more proof."

"How are we going to get that?" Mitch asked.

"You need to see your birth certificates," she nodded wisely, "they have your father's name on them."

"How can we do that?" I wrote.

Cora thought for a moment.

"I know, tell your Mum that Mr. Philpot needs them to update the school records."

It was a good idea and I think we may have tried it out if something else had not occurred. Just as we rounded the corner near to where our den had been, who should we see but Mr. Mitchell! The three of them all yelled his name at once and Mr. Mitchell, who had had his back to us and seemed to be examining the hedge, whirled around with a look of shock on his face. It was quickly replaced by a smile however and he walked over to us.

"Hi," he said, "what are you four up to?"

We explained that we'd been for a walk.

"Well," he said, "it's good to take exercise, been doing the same myself as a matter of fact, but hadn't you better be getting along home? It'll be dark in half an hour."

We agreed, of course. Cora said goodbye and turned back. Mr. Mitchell went off down Church Lane. Johnny, Mitch and I continued walking towards our houses but our curiosity was aroused.

"What do you think he was doing?" Johnny asked.

Mitch sighed. "What he said - walking."

"But," Johnny persisted, "shouldn't he be at school, working?"

"I expect he needed some fresh air."

This was so obvious that Johnny and I had to agree with him.

By the time we got home Mum was back from work. Mitch and I looked at one another. Of course, Mr. Mitchell had been hoping to meet her.

Mitch said innocently, "Did you see Mr. Mitchell by the bus stop, Mum?"

"No," Mum replied, a slight frown on her face, "why?"

"We just met him in the lane. He said he was going for a walk."

"Well, there you are then," Mum said, "but I didn't see him."

Nothing more was said that evening but Mitch and I spent a long time when we were supposed to be asleep writing to each other in my book. There was so much to think about. Should we try to see our birth certificates or ask Mum or even Mr. Mitchell if he was our father? Would it upset Gran and Granddad? What would our friends think? I also had my own private worries about the second Peter photograph and what Mrs. Clay would think of my letter. It was all very confusing and, if I'm honest, it made me very nervous.

That Sunday was Remembrance Sunday, the day when we remembered Uncle Peter and all the other servicemen from our village who had been killed in both wars. Before Sunday school started the whole village, including Cora's family, assembled around the Memorial in the churchyard. All the men who had been killed fighting had their names inscribed on it. There was a long list of names from the First War but only one from the last war - Uncle Peter's. It was a very sad day for our family. Graham Parker's father played the Last Post on his cornet, the vicar prayed, wreaths were laid and wooden sticks with poppies on them were planted around the Memorial. Then we all sang "Abide With Me". As we left to go into the church, I saw Gran run her fingers over Uncle Peter's inscription. That made me feel very sad as I knew she missed him terribly.

Mrs. Clay asked me to remain behind after Sunday school. She told the others I had written a question but she needed to know more about what I was thinking so she could answer more fully and that it would take a while for me to write things down. That was quite true of course. I think the others, especially Mitch, were slightly surprised but they must have thought it was about last week's story so they went off happily enough. When we were alone, Mrs. Clay took my letter out of her bag.

"Now, Josie, first of all I'm glad you wrote to me."

I couldn't help giving a sigh of relief. We had a good conversation about my growing-up worries. She was so reassuring, telling me she had had the same worries at my age although she understood mine were different owing to my condition and perhaps I was more than usually worried because of that. However, she said Mr. Philpot would tell the new school about my difficulties so that they would be ready to help me the same as he had been. She said the teachers would tell the other girls in my class so they would know they would have to be patient with me. She also said that she had a friend who had been to a boarding school and had quite enjoyed it but, because of my problem, my Mum would never let me go away to school. I was so relieved.

Then, quite casually, she said, "Why exactly are you concerned about Mr. Mitchell? Is it because your Mum went to the dance with him or because he said what you took for a German word?"

"Both," I wrote.

"I see," she said, and waited.

I couldn't help it, I had to tell her that Mitch and I wondered if he was our long-lost father but that I hadn't really taken to him and how much Granddad would hate it if our father turned out to be an American.

She just said, "I see," again, rather thoughtfully, and then said, "Come on, I'll walk you home and I promise not to say anything about your ideas about your father."

Although dinner was ready when we got there, Mrs. Clay spent a short time in the front room talking privately to Mum. This time Gran didn't eavesdrop and made sure Mitch and I couldn't either. Granddad had gone out for a before-dinner pint at the pub with Johnny's dad and was just a minute or so too late to see Mrs. Clay. I thought Mum was slightly odd throughout dinner; there was a sort of false brightness about her but we were all listening to a comedy show on the wireless as we ate and no-one else seemed to notice.

Days went by and we were beginning to get excited by the fact that it would soon be Christmas and school holidays. We heard that Stinky Jim was out of the nursing home and going around the villages again. Everything, it seemed, had returned to normal so it was a shock to get home from school one afternoon to find we had a visitor. We never had visitors. Gran met us half-way down the lane and explained that an old friend of Mum's had come to see her and us too.

"Who is she?" Mitch asked, "Why does she want to see us?"

Gran said, "Them that asks no questions gets told no lies" and wouldn't say more.

Mum and the visitor were in the front room. So was Granddad. Gran made us wash our hands and faces at the kitchen sink and brush our hair before we were allowed in. Gran carried in one of the kitchen chairs so that there was room for everybody to sit down. Mum was on the settee where we joined her. Granddad sat on the kitchen chair holding his useless arm in his good hand and Gran sat in an armchair. In the other armchair sat the visitor. She was quite a bit older than Mum but round and cuddly, just like Mrs. Clay. She had her hat and coat off and an empty cup and saucer stood by her chair so we knew that she had been there some time. Her hair was dark and naturally curly and her eyes were kind. As we came in, she gave us a big smile.

"Hello, Mitch and Josie. I'm Mrs. Mason, although I used to be called Nurse Josephine Mitchell."

Chapter 5

For a moment, the world stopped. She was Nurse Josephine Mitchell! So Mum hadn't made her up, she was real, which meant we really had been named after her! We must have looked as astonished as we felt because Mum quickly took over.

"Mrs. Mason and I have kept in touch ever since you were born. She has always wanted to meet you, especially now you're growing up so fast."

I really couldn't see what that had to do with it but Mum did seem quite on edge so I guessed there was more to come. She put her arms around us, hugging us close, and then said, "You see, Mrs. Mason knows all about your father and we think it's time you should know the truth too."

Mitch couldn't help himself. He blurted out, "Mr. Mitchell's our Dad, isn't he?"

Now it was Gran and Granddad's turn to look astonished but Mum just shook her head.

"That's really why Mrs. Mason and I have decided you should all know the truth, before things got out of hand."

"What are you talking about?" asked Granddad.
Mum looked at him.

"The children have got the idea into their heads that their teacher is their father. I don't know why."

Mitch was outraged and I felt a little sick. Had Mrs. Clay gone back on her promise and told Mum about our conversation?

"Did Johnny blab?" Mitch asked.

"Not exactly," Mum replied, "I don't expect you know that Johnny sometimes talks in his sleep?"

We shook our heads.

"His Aunt Delia heard him a couple of nights ago, saying in his sleep that you all thought that Mr. Mitchell was your father so she came and told me. I was quite shocked that you should think that."

"But Mum," Mitch said, "you went to the dance with him. Why would you do that if he's not our father?"

"I had my reasons," Mum said, "but if you'll be quiet for a moment I'll ask Mrs. Mason to tell you about your real father."

"Why can't you tell us?" I wrote.

Mrs. Mason butted in."It's quite a sad story and your mother may get upset before she can finish telling you everything. So is it alright if I begin?"

Granddad said, "I think you'd better." He looked quite grim.

The things Mrs. Mason told us were so unexpected that we were left open-mouthed. She told us that Mum had been a clever young woman and had got a place at a secretarial college in London to study shorthand and typing. It meant that she had to live in a boarding house during the week as it would have been too difficult to travel up to London each day. While she was in London she met a young man who was also living at the boarding house. After a while they fell in love and because it was during the war, things became topsy-turvy and we were born before they could get married. I was shocked at first but then remembered that things were different at that time. After all, all sorts of strange things happened during the war. She then said our father was also very clever and had in fact been chosen to go on a secret mission to France.

Mitch really sat up then.

"Do you mean he was a spy?" he gasped.

"Yes, sort of," Mrs. Mason agreed, "he was very brave and joined the French freedom fighters. He went on several highly secret missions that saved lots of lives but sadly he was betrayed and died."

It took a minute or two for this information to sink in.

Then Mitch said sadly, "So our father is dead?"

"Yes, I'm sorry Mitch. If he had lived he would have married your mother and you would have had a good father. However, you can feel very, very proud of him and I'm sure he would have been proud of you and would have loved you as much as he loved your Mum."

I wrote, "What was his name?"

Mrs. Mason looked at Mum. Mum cleared her throat and looked straight at Granddad.

"His name," she said, "was Peter Schultz, and I loved him."

Thinking back to that afternoon, it was as well Mrs. Mason was in the room or goodness knows what might have happened. As soon as Mum mentioned our father's German surname Granddad, whose face was bright red, leapt up so suddenly from his chair that it toppled over with a crash. Gran jumped up and tried to restrain him but she grabbed his strong, good arm and he easily shook her off.

Mum still had her arms around us but I felt her shrink back. Granddad was trying to say something but he couldn't get his words out. He was very, very angry. Mitch and I jumped up too, more frightened than we'd ever been. Mitch gave a cry, and threw himself between Granddad and Mum.

"Don't hurt her, don't hurt my Mum!"

The only calm person in the room was Mrs. Mason. Without getting up and in a normal voice she said, "Mr. Sutton, please sit down. I know all this is a shock, but you don't know the whole truth yet."

Granddad turned on her.

"What is there to know?" he yelled.

"You're telling me my daughter went with a ruddy German in the middle of the war and I'm supposed to take it quietly? What do you take me for - a mouse?"

Mrs. Mason's voice changed. It became sterner and louder.

"Have you not heard a word I've been saying, Mr. Sutton? I've just told you that Peter Schultz was a war hero."

Granddad was still raving. "Oh, yes, on whose side though? I'm not having a Nazi collaborator under my roof! She can go - right now!"

We were all crying; Mum, Mitch and me. Even Gran had tears in her eyes.

Mrs. Mason stood up and raised her voice, just like Mr. Philpot does if someone is really misbehaving.

"Mr. Sutton! You are behaving like an idiot! If you don't pick up that chair and sit down and show some decorum, I'll call the police!"

Granddad's chest was heaving, but he sat down.

"This is my house," he said, rather feebly, "you can't come in here and threaten me …"

Then he did something that frightened us even more. He began to sob.

It's a terrible thing to see an adult sobbing. Granddad's face sort of crumpled, his nose was running and he was pulling at his hair. Gran knelt beside him and tried to comfort him and Mum kept saying, "I'm sorry, I'm sorry," over and over.

Mrs. Mason said quietly to Gran, "I'm going to make us all a cup of tea and then we'll talk this over once we've all calmed down."

Then turning to us, "Would you two come with me and show me where the tea things are kept?"

Shaking, we obeyed. By the time the kettle had boiled and we had set cups and saucers ready on the tray, Mrs. Mason had calmed us down. She explained that Granddad was in shock and although Uncle Peter had died many years ago he was also crying because he had lost his only son.

When we went back into the front room with the tea things, Granddad was wiping his face with his handkerchief and Gran was sitting on the settee with her arm around Mum.

As Mrs. Mason sat down again, Gran looked up and said to Granddad, "Now, Bill, are you ready to hear Mrs. Mason out?"

Granddad nodded, but Mrs. Mason said, "I'll pour the tea first, it will help to have a breathing space."

I wondered at the fact that Gran didn't bristle at being ordered about in her own home but she seemed content to let Mrs. Mason take the lead. Mum was still weepy so with her permission Mrs. Mason told us the rest of the story.

Peter Schultz was only half German; his mother was English. His father had been a newspaper journalist in Berlin and when Adolf Hitler became the leader of Germany Peter's father realised that he would soon become a terrible dictator. Here she paused and said to Granddad, "Not all Germans are Nazis, you know".

Mr. Schultz quickly brought his family to England and got a job in London. When the war started even though he hated the Nazis, as he was a German citizen he had to give up his work and live in a sort of camp, in case he turned out to be a German spy. There was talk that Peter should be sent there too but then Peter volunteered to be sent into France as a secret agent. He could, of course, speak perfect German and very good French too. He was cleared by the security forces and began his training. Mrs. Mason said we know now that when he was living in the boarding house and met Mum he had nearly finished his training. Soon after he was parachuted into France, which was occupied by the German army, and lived there in secret, fighting the enemy undercover. As she had told us, unfortunately he was betrayed and was shot by the Nazis. He was just twenty-one years old.

Mum was really crying now but I remembered the second Peter photograph and understood. I had never known that grown-ups could have secrets, let alone my own mother. Somehow it made me feel closer to her than ever. Sometimes secrets are kept for good reasons. Our father, Peter, would have had to keep very many secrets or we might have lost the war, and Mum kept his identity secret because she knew how upset Granddad would be. I decided there and then that it would not be a terrible thing if I kept secret, even from Mitch, the fact that I had been in Mum's bedroom and found the photograph she'd hidden for years.

Mrs. Mason had to catch the last bus back to Ashwood, where she was staying the night, but she promised she would come again "if I'm allowed to", looking at Granddad. He didn't say yes but he didn't say no. We were given a late supper and sent to bed but we lay listening to the murmur of the adults' voices for a very long time. I don't think anyone in the house slept much that night. It was as if we had all had the same peculiar dream.

In the morning, Mum asked us to keep the secret of our real father for a little longer until we'd all got used to the idea, but she did give us permission to tell Johnny and Cora that she had told us that Mr. Mitchell definitely wasn't our father. I told her about Cora's idea of looking at our birth certificates so she fetched them for us. The space under 'father's name' was blank.

"So you see," she said, "you can truthfully say that you've seen your birth certificates and that your father's name was not on them."

It was hard to have to go into school the next day. We were tired and confused and quite unable to take in all that had happened. When Johnny called for us he wanted to know what all the shouting had been about in our house the afternoon before.

We live in a semi-detached cottage; Johnny's family lives in the other half so that if there is any loud noise in one house the people living in the attached cottage can hear it. Thankfully Johnny's family couldn't hear what was actually said but they could tell something was going on. We said Granddad and Mum had had a bad argument but that they had made it up now. Johnny accepted that, but we could tell we hadn't satisfied his curiosity.

"You two look odd" he said.

I wrote, "We didn't sleep too well after the row. We were worried Mum and Granddad wouldn't make up."

Johnny said, "Yes, I can see that. I'd be worried if Mum and Aunt Delia had a row but they never have."

"You're lucky," Mitch said glumly.

It was hard too to face Mr. Mitchell. I was glad he wasn't our father but I think Mitch was a little disappointed, even though we were so proud our real father had been a hero. It would have been wonderful to find that our father was still alive and coming to find us. Mr. Mitchell could see that we weren't ourselves that day and although he didn't say anything we could see him watching us. When school was over he kept us back.

"Is anything the matter?" he asked, "Your minds seemed to be wandering today."

I didn't know what to say, but Mitch was quicker on the uptake and told him the same story that we'd told

51

Johnny, that Mum and Granddad had had a bad argument and it had upset us so much we couldn't sleep.

Mr. Mitchell was thoughtful.

"Hmm," he said, "I hope it wasn't on account of me."

Mitch said, "Oh no, I don't think so."

Mr. Mitchell walked with us to the school gate. As we reached it we could see Stinky Jim trudging down the lane. He looked a little less unkempt than usual as he was wearing a slightly newer coat and cap.

"Getting cold now." Mr. Mitchell said, "Hope old baldy there has somewhere warm to sleep. Well, get along home, you two."

He gave us a sort of salute and went off towards the bus stop. We turned in the opposite direction and started for home, when suddenly it came to me just what Mr. Mitchell had said, and I stopped dead.

"What?" asked Mitch.

I grabbed his arm so tightly that he yelled.

"Ow! Why'd you do that?"

I held my nose and sketched a capital M in the air, our signs for Stinky Jim and Mr. Mitchell.

"What about them?" Mitch asked.

Quickly, I scribbled, "He called Stinky Jim baldy."

"So?" Mitch queried.

"So," I wrote, "how did he know Stinky Jim was bald?"

Mitch hunched his shoulders. "Why shouldn't he?"

"Because," I wrote, "nobody had ever seen Jim without his cap until he was attacked. You remember how surprised we were to see that he was bald?"

Mitch turned to me, his mouth open. Then he closed it and said, "Well, somebody must have told him."

"Why would they?" I countered, "Why would anyone think he'd be interested?"

"You can't think ..." Mitch began, but of course I did.

What if it had been Mr. Mitchell who'd attacked Stinky Jim? And if so, why? We agreed then and there that there was something strange about our teacher, things, as Granddad would have put it, that didn't add up. We would have to keep an eye on him.

Chapter 6

Cora's mother was going to have another baby. Cora was praying to Jesus, Mary and Joseph that it would be a girl. Because of this we didn't see so much of Cora after school. Her father worked on a different farm to Granddad, one that had sheep, and he often had to work into the evening. Mrs. Murphy wasn't feeling very well and she needed Cora to help look after her brothers so we were really surprised to find Cora waiting outside our gate before school one morning. She was hopping up and down with excitement and could hardly wait for Johnny to join us before letting us in on her news.

"Guess what?" she said, "I saw Horrendous Hicks last night - here, in the village!"

"Oh no!" the boys chorused.

None of us wanted her back. Then Cora told us what had happened at her house the evening before. Her youngest brother had eaten some wizened rosehips that he'd picked from the hedgerow and had been sick. Her mother had been sick, too, even though she hadn't eaten the rosehips. Mr. Murphy was still up at the farm so Cora, even though it was past bedtime, had taken charge. Sometimes the water supply to their cottage isn't very reliable. Last night was one of those times, so Cora had to brave the dark in order to get a bucket of water from the old pump in their yard. She had just finished and was about to get back to the house as quickly as she could when she noticed a bicycle light approaching. Thinking it was her father back from work, she ran to the gate. To her surprise, the cyclist rode straight past without seeing her. However, the woman on the bicycle was caught in the light from the kitchen window and Cora immediately recognised Miss Hicks! She watched her turn into Church Lane and ride towards the school.

None of us doubted that Cora had really seen Miss Hicks; we'd all seen her on her bicycle often enough, and dreaded that she was back for good. Her father must be better, we thought, or dead. We went into school in fear and trepidation, but as usual Mr. Mitchell was sitting at the teacher's desk and there was no sign of Horrendous. All day we waited for Mr. Philpot to come in and tell us that she was coming back but he never did. We were stumped. If she wasn't coming back to school, what was she doing riding down Church Lane at that time of night when she was supposed to be nursing her father? It was time for a serious talk. It was no good going for a walk for we might bump into Mr. Mitchell again or even Miss Hicks. There was only one place we could meet - back at the old den.

Because it was getting dark earlier and earlier, we had to wait for Saturday to come before we could meet. Even then, it was the afternoon as we all had chores to do first, but we were free after dinner. It felt strange to tread the familiar path. It seemed that no-one had been there since Stinky Jim had been taken to hospital, the remains of his broken beer bottle were still scattered around. We didn't go into the den itself, but stood outside it.

Johnny said, "What do you think is going on? Mr. Mitchell's not your father, so why has he come to our little village? Why was Horrendous cycling to the school in the dark if she wasn't going to see Mr. Philpot? And who knocked out Stinky Jim and why?"

Cora borrowed my notebook.

"Right," she said, resting the notebook against a tree, "let's look at this logically. Number one: Horrendous Hicks. She's not there when we go back to school at the end of the summer holidays because her father is ill and she

55

has to look after him. She doesn't live in the village so why was she cycling to the school on Tuesday night? Number two: Mr. Mitchell. He comes to take Miss Hicks's place at short notice. Why did he take a job in our little village and not in one of the schools in the towns? Number three: Stinky Jim. Who attacked him and why and how did Mr. Mitchell know he is bald?"

Mitch said, "There are probably logical answers. Horrendous may have left something at school that she needed, there might not have been any jobs in the town schools for Mr. Mitchell and someone may have told him that Stinky Jim is bald."

I shook my head and wrote, "This could be serious. We should tell someone."

"Like who?" Mitch asked, "They'll only come to the same conclusions."

"We need more proof. We need to keep a watch for Horrendous Hicks and follow her," Johnny said.

"Don't be daft," said Mitch, "how can we keep watch every evening? Anyway, she might not have anything to do with Stinky or Mr. Mitchell."

We fell silent, then Cora said, "Then we'll just have to follow Mr. Mitchell instead."

Soon we had devised a rota. We would start our watch the following week. Mitch and Johnny had football practice after school on Mondays so they could keep watch then and Cora had choir practice on Tuesday, so then it would be her turn. I volunteered to find some excuse to stay after school on Wednesday. We would have to sort out the rest of the week later.

Mitch and Johnny found it difficult to keep watch on their day. They explained to Cora and me how Mr. Philpot, who took football, had them practising shooting at the far end of the field from the school gates. Mitch was in goal, his usual position, and Johnny was about to take his first shot when, out of the corner of his eye, Mitch saw Mr. Mitchell walking towards the school gates. Quickly, he signalled to Johnny who half-turned just as his boot struck the ball so that his shot went wide. Mr. Philpot groaned and told him to have another go. Mitch's eyes were still on the gate and distracted Johnny, whose second shot also went wide.

The other boys couldn't understand it. Johnny was the school's leading goal scorer and never missed a penalty. Mr. Philpot was exasperated.

"What's wrong with you, boy? Last week you were Stanley Matthews and this week you're Coco the Clown!"

The other boys laughed and Mitch and Johnny snapped back into being footballers. Johnny's next shot nearly took Mitch's head off but they had lost sight of Mr. Mitchell.

Cora had better luck. As the school choir was to take part in the church's carol service Miss Napier (who took everyone for singing) had arranged for them to have a rehearsal in the church itself so that, she said, they could get used to the acoustics. She made it sound as though the choir was to perform in the Albert Hall but in fact our church is not particularly big. The entrance is through a thick oak door at the front which leads into the main body of the church. There are several rows of pews divided by an aisle which finishes at the altar, above which is a splendid stained-glass window. On either side of the altar are an organ and a small room called the vestry, which is where we have Sunday school. Behind the pews is a marble christening font and behind that the most interesting thing of all, the bell tower. There is a full length, very thick curtain barring the entrance to the tower. We were never allowed behind it, as Mrs. Clay said the stairs up to the top are dangerous but of course we'd often peeped. There wasn't much to see at ground level, just the bottom steps and the bell rope which hangs from the ceiling high above. It is coloured red and blue and coiled up on itself so we couldn't have reached it even if we'd tried. From outside the tower is square and solid looking. In the church guide book it says it has a crenellated parapet and in the centre of the tower hangs the bell, attached to a sort of solid iron trestle with a wooden canopy over it. It is only rung on special occasions so we hadn't heard it very often. When it is rung it swings the whole width of the tower. No other church in the district has one like it and people come from all over to photograph it.

Miss Napier marched the choir members into the church immediately school was over. It was a chilly early December afternoon and they buried their cold noses in their scarves. It was cold in the church too so they were allowed to keep their coats on but Miss Napier made them take off their scarves. Then she arranged them in order of height so that Cora was in the back row. Miss Napier couldn't play the organ so they had to sing unaccompanied.

After half-an-hour of a shaky 'Silent Night' and a not-quite-in-tune 'While Shepherds Watched' Cora said they'd all had enough, even Miss Napier, so she let them go.

Cora was one of the last to file out and as she got to the church door she heard Miss Napier call, "Why, Mr. Mitchell! I'm afraid we've finished our rehearsal!"

Cora saw Mr. Mitchell straighten up from a rather fine tomb he had been examining in the graveyard, and walk towards them.

She heard him answer, "Isn't that a shame? I heard lovely singing from the school so I thought I'd come and listen."

Miss Napier was all of a twitter, fluttering her eyelashes and fussing with her hair. She didn't give another glance to the remaining girls and walked off with Mr. Mitchell.

On her way home, a thought lodged itself in Cora's mind and the next morning at break she got us together. After telling us about the afternoon's happenings, she said, "If you think about it, how could Mr. Mitchell have heard the singing from the church if he was still in school? It's too far away, and the organ wasn't playing. So why was he in the churchyard?"

"Perhaps he wanted to meet Miss Napier," said Johnny.

"Don't be daft," Mitch retorted. "Not with all the girls there. What do you think, Josie?"

I couldn't think of any furtive reason why Mr. Mitchell would have been in the graveyard either but something else did come to mind.

"Cora," I wrote, "when you saw Miss Hicks, are you sure she cycled all the way to the school?"

Cora frowned. "Well, no, of course not, you know the lane bends and anyway it was dark."

I was excited. "Maybe she was meeting Mr. Mitchell in the churchyard."

The others laughed.

"You're mad!" Cora, who was frightened of ghosts, said. "Who would go to the churchyard after dark? Anyway, they don't know each other."

I was put out. I had been serious, but I had to agree my idea wasn't exactly logical.

It was my turn next to keep an eye on our teacher. We'd agreed that Mitch would tell Gran that I was staying behind to help Miss Blake, the infant teacher, to sort out the costumes for the infants' nativity play. In a way it wasn't altogether a lie as I'd done just that at lunchtime. What I had also done was to persuade Mr. Philpot to let me cut some holly from a hedge near the school and arrange it in the vases as the flowers I had been watering had died from old age. I spent a long time selecting bits of holly to cut. Thankfully, just as I was getting really cold and ready to give up, Mr. Mitchell walked out of the school gates carrying his briefcase and set off down the lane towards the main road and the bus stop. I followed slowly, ready with a plausible excuse should he turn and see me. What I hadn't bargained for was Mr. Philpot leaving school early for once. I was so intent on walking slowly and yet keeping Mr. Mitchell in sight that the sound of his car approaching from behind had me jumping out of my skin. The car stopped and Mr. Philpot put his head out of the window.

"Come on, Josie, it's too cold to gather holly. Hop in and I'll run you home." With that he leaned across and opened the passenger door. I couldn't very well refuse and normally I would have been thrilled for the opportunity of a ride. I scrambled in, trying to see where Mr. Mitchell had got to. We soon caught up with him. Mr. Philpot honked the horn and Mr. Mitchell stopped.

"Just giving Josie here a lift home then I'll pick you up," Mr. Philpot yelled as we slowed down.

Mr. Mitchell nodded and gave us one of his salutes.

"Well," said Johnny as we trudged to school the following morning, "fine lot of spies we turned out to be."

"I saw something," Cora said.

"Yes," Johnny replied, "but seeing Mr. Mitchell in the churchyard is hardly earth-shattering, is it?"

Mitch sighed. "Maybe there isn't any mystery after all; maybe we just want there to be one."

I wrote nothing. Mitch was probably right. I sat down at my desk and reached into my schoolbag for pens and pencils, ready for the first lesson of the day. That was when I got my first shock. I carry two notebooks with me to school, one for school stuff and a private one for conversations with friends. As I felt in the bag I realised only one book was there. Hastily I pulled it out. Oh, no! It was the blue one, the school one, which meant the red notebook, the one with 'Josie Sutton - PRIVATE' written on the cover was missing. Frantically I signalled to Mitch. Mr. Mitchell noticed.

"Something wrong, Josie?" he asked, without smiling.

Mitch said, "She's lost her notebook sir."

Mr. Mitchell didn't know I had two notebooks.

He said, "No big deal. Lots of paper here."

He slapped some sheets down on the desk in front of me.

"You can write all you need to on that."

There was something in the way he said "all you need to" that made the hairs on the back of my neck stand on end. It sounded threatening.

When school was over he asked me to wait behind. Mitch offered to wait too but Mr. Mitchell said not to bother, he wouldn't keep me long. Once everyone had left the classroom Mr. Mitchell went to his desk and opened a drawer. Looking at me with a strange, unreadable expression he pulled out my missing red notebook and threw it across to me.

"You dropped it in Mr. Philpot's car," he said. "I found it. I said I would return it to you."

He looked quite angry. He walked across to me and stood very close, looking down at me. I was truly frightened, he'd never looked angry before.

"Now listen here, Miss Busybody. You and your brother and your friends should stop playing at detectives before you get yourselves into real trouble. Nobody likes being talked about, especially when the talk is all lies. Now git."

I didn't need a second bidding. I grabbed my notebook and my schoolbag and ran all the way towards home, catching up with the others just as they reached Cora's house. They could see at once that I was frightened and crowded around me.

"What's up? What happened?" they demanded but I was too shaken to write anything. Instead, I showed them the notebook.

"Did Mr. Mitchell find it?" Cora asked.

I nodded miserably.

"Oh," Mitch said, catching on, "he didn't read it, did he?"

I nodded again and couldn't help crying.

"Right," said Mitch, manfully, "we could be in trouble. This time we do tell Mum."

Mum was horrified that Mr. Mitchell had made me cry. She wanted to go up to the school immediately and complain to Mr. Philpot but we begged her not to. More gently, she asked what was in my notebook to make Mr. Mitchell so angry. Shamefaced, Mitch gave her a brief outline of our worries - we couldn't really call them suspicions. Suspicions about what?

Gran, who was listening, said, "See where tittle tattle will get you?"

Mum said, ignoring Gran, "Josie, would you let me see your notebook? I would like to understand what you have all been saying before I see Mr. Philpot."

I looked at Mitch. After all, it wasn't just my thoughts written there but his and Johnny's and Cora's too. Mitch hesitated and then nodded, so I handed over the incriminating red notebook.

Much to my relief, Mr. Mitchell was absent from school the next day. Mr. Philpot came to teach us, telling us that Mr. Mitchell was unwell but would be back on Monday. I heard Johnny give a sort of snort and Cora whispered, "It should be us who are unwell."

I blushed, for I had thought about having a pretend stomach ache in order to stay at home and not confront Mr. Mitchell but Gran always knows when we are genuinely sick. As we passed the churchyard on the way home, Mrs. Clay saw us and waved. We stopped and she came over to us.

"Would you help me with something?" she said, "Cora, I believe you noticed that Mr. Mitchell was interested in one of the tombs in the churchyard. Would you be able to point it out to me? Then I could find out more about it for him."

How did she know? Had Mum read it in my notebook and told her? She must have done. We went into the churchyard with her but Cora couldn't decide which tomb it had been.

"Where were you when you saw Mr. Mitchell?" Mrs. Clay asked.

Cora went to stand by the church door and then she remembered.

"That one!" she said, pointing.

"Are you sure?" Mrs. Clay asked and Cora nodded.

Mrs. Clay went over to the tomb and examined it.

"Oh, yes, this is an interesting one," she said and stood up. "Thank you for your help."

I was convinced she had quickly removed something from the ledge under the lid of the tomb but she didn't say anything about that. I told the others but no-one else had noticed.

Saturday proved to be very wet, a miserable stay-indoors sort of day. However Cora's mother was unwell again, and as her father was up at the farm, she volunteered to go to the shop. She dressed in her old waterproof windcheater which had a hood she could wear against the wind and rain. While she was waiting her turn to be served, the local bus pulled up opposite. She looked through the window to see who was boarding it and who was getting off. Mr. Mitchell got off. He was wearing a long raincoat with the collar turned up and a wide-brimmed hat and had his back to the shop but she was sure it was him. The rain was coming down in sheets and he had his head down.

"Yes, Cora?" asked the shopkeeper, "What can I get for you?"

Quickly Cora thrust her mother's shopping list into his hand and said, "This please. I'll be back soon," and with that she ran out of the shop, leaving the shop keeper open mouthed. She was just in time to see Mr. Mitchell turn towards the church and then she ran back up our lane. Mitch opened the door to her and seeing her soaking wet and out of breath, called me. Mum and Gran were upstairs changing bed sheets and Granddad was in the shed. Quickly Cora blurted out her news. She went to fetch Johnny while I grabbed our coats and Wellington boots and Mitch called upstairs, "Just going round to Johnny's," and we were out the door. I thought I heard Mum call back, "What?" but didn't stop to answer her.

Because of the rain the churchyard was deserted but for one figure. We crept up by the hedge which bordered the entrance porch where we could just see Mr. Mitchell. He was standing by the tomb Cora had pointed out to Mrs. Clay, probing the ledge with his fingers. Whatever he was looking for obviously wasn't there; we heard him swear and bend down to look more closely.

Mitch tapped me on the shoulder. He put his mouth close to my ear and whispered, "Come on, we need to tell on him."

I shook my head, pointed to my mouth and then Mr. Mitchell. Then I pointed to my ears and eyes. Mitch understood. I couldn't make a sound so wasn't likely to give myself away by coughing or crying out. I would be the perfect spy.

"O.K," he whispered," you can keep lookout but make sure he doesn't see you."

My heart thumping, I watched as Mr. Mitchell searched all around the tomb, feeling it all over and digging his fingers into cracks. He swore again. This time I was sure using the same German word he had used on Bonfire Night. Then he straightened up and seemed to look directly at me. I held my breath and ducked lower. Slowly I brought my head up and saw him turn towards the church. He was walking out of my line of vision and the rain was running down my face so I had to crane my neck to see. That was my undoing. I was wearing Wellington boots. They were flat and had no tread on the soles and the path by the hedge was by now very muddy indeed. My foot slipped and, caught off-balance, I fell and crashed through the hedge.

He was on me in seconds. Hauling me up by the arm he spat out, "Little Miss Busybody, spying again."

My face and hands were scratched and bleeding. His face was contorted. I was terrified; what would he do? Then we both heard the approaching sound of a police car, bell clanging. He looked around wildly then, picking me up bodily, he ran to the church door. I struggled desperately and one of my Wellingtons fell off. Dropping me on the hard paving inside, he slammed the heavy door shut. I had never noticed that it was possible to bolt the door from the inside but he was obviously aware of this and shot the bolts into place. As I was picking myself up he turned to me and grabbed me again.

"You will be most useful," he said.

I certainly did not like the sound of that. Then there was the cacophony of more police cars arriving, their bells clanging madly. The rain was easing off at last and I could hear the sound of someone in authority shouting orders. The windows in the body of the church are too high up to see through, even for Mr. Mitchell. A furious pounding began on the oak door but it was far too strong for anyone to force it open. Mr. Mitchell was muttering to himself. He seemed to have forgotten about me and I started to creep towards the door. He saw me, of course.

"No you don't," he said. Then, "What's behind that curtain?"

Of course I couldn't answer him, even if I cared to. He hauled me up and pulled back part of the curtain.

"Of course," he said aloud, "the bell tower!"With that, he pushed me behind the curtain and followed quickly.

"Up the steps" he commanded, but I remembered Mrs. Clay saying they were unsafe and hesitated.

"Do as I say!" he yelled, giving me a vicious kick.

If I could have screamed I would have but I managed to climb the steps, Mr. Mitchell close behind me. We emerged on to the roof of the bell tower in front of the large brass bell. There wasn't much room to get past it but Mr. Mitchell put his arm around my chest and shoulders and holding me tightly marched me to the edge of the parapet, looking down on the churchyard. I was wet through and the foot without a boot on it was soaked and painfully cold. The rain had eased at last and a crowd had gathered, fronted by several policemen. I could see Mum looking frantically up at us and Constable Banks holding her back. A policeman in a peaked hat with braid on his shoulders called up to Mr. Mitchell.

"Don't be a fool!" he shouted. "There's no way out. Let the girl go and come out, or we will have to batter the door in."

Mr. Mitchell reached into his pocket with his free hand and to my horror pulled out a gun.

"Oh yeah?" he replied, "I think this might change your mind."

He pointed the gun at the policeman, who retreated a step or two. Then he waved the gun at me and shouted, "Don't think I won't use it either."

I heard Mum scream and then suddenly there was Mitch, running towards the church with Constable Banks in pursuit.

Mr Mitchell, jumpy as he was, yelled, "No nearer! No nearer!"

And then he shot Mitch.

Chapter 7

All was confusion after that. I think Mr. Mitchell was as shocked as I was. He let go of me and I slumped down to the rain-puddled floor. I was shaking all over and tears were running down my face. I badly wanted to be with Mitch, to sign that I loved him.

Mr. Mitchell backed away muttering, "The policeman - I aimed for the policeman."

He was standing with his back to the staircase when suddenly I heard a familiar voice from inside the church yell, "Duck, Josie, duck!"

I lowered my head just as the bell started to swing on its cradle. There was a long, loud doooong as the clapper hit the inside of the bell as it swung towards Mr. Mitchell. He half turned and fired his gun downwards into the church. Then the bell caught him and knocked him down the steps. All I remember after that is being carried carefully down those same steps by Constable Banks. When we reached the bottom he tried to shield my eyes but I had already seen two bodies stretched out on the floor of the bell tower – those of Mr. Mitchell and Mrs. Clay. There was a lot of blood. Ambulance men were kneeling down looking at them. One man was saying, "She's still alive, but he's a gonner."

Mrs. Clay had been shot in the head but thankfully not fatally. She had acted very swiftly and bravely to try to save me. During the confusion after Mitch was shot, she had run around to the back of the church. Everyone had forgotten the narrow door which led directly into the vestry.

It was kept locked but being the Sunday school teacher she had a key. She had let herself in and crept quietly to the bottom of the bell chamber. She would have had to jump to reach the bell rope which was probably when she shouted up to me to duck. She would have known Mr. Mitchell couldn't have dodged out of the way once the bell started to swing. Sadly the one shot he had managed to fire had hit her. She was in a coma for days and when she came round she couldn't talk very well or move her right arm or leg.

It was some weeks before everyone knew the full story of what had been going on. Mitch was taken to the hospital. He wasn't badly hurt. Mr. Mitchell's bullet had hit him in the arm. It was what is called a flesh wound. In other words it didn't break any bones so that although it hurt Mitch a lot there wasn't any lasting damage. He had to have his arm in a sling for a few weeks, though, and is always showing off the scar. He said he'd been running towards the church because he meant to climb the outside of the tower and save me. Mum told me she thought he was mortified that he'd left me alone with Mr. Mitchell and that he was trying to make up for it. I was made to stay in bed for the rest of the week. Everyone came to see me, even Miss Napier. Mr. Philpot gave me a brand new notebook and Constable Banks had made a Certificate of Bravery for me. Doctor Simmonds came regularly to check on me and it was he who told me about the newspaper reporters and photographers who had invaded the village. They had wanted to speak to me and take my photograph but he had told them I was in shock and couldn't be interviewed. Was I? I suppose for a couple of days I was. I couldn't do anything, just slept a lot and cuddled my old teddy. I had terrible dreams too. Mum and Gran and even Granddad fussed over me. Mitch and Johnny and Cora came up to see me every day and before long I was worrying to be allowed up. Doctor Simmonds gave me permission and laughingly said something to Mum about the resilience of children.

Once Mrs. Clay was out of danger there was a meeting at the school as there was no village hall. Everybody went. The concertina doors between our classroom and Miss Napier's had been folded back to make room for everyone. Two teachers' desks had been pushed together at one end of the hall, and Mr. Philpot, Constable Banks, the vicar and Doctor Simmonds, as the most important men in the village, sat behind them. There was a lot of murmuring as people filed in and took their places on the rows of chairs but the atmosphere was subdued. Cora, Johnny, Mitch and I sat with our families on the front row, Mitch still with his arm in a sling. Mr. Philpot started the proceedings by stating the purpose of the meeting was to inform the villagers of what had led up to the siege of the bell tower, as he called it, and the unfortunate death of Mr. Mitchell. Some of what was said after that frankly went over our heads but people were allowed to ask questions and it was from the answers given that we at last understood - and there was one revelation that left us all stunned.

The whole business was connected with the war. Mr. Mitchell, although an American citizen, was of German descent and very proud of the fact. He had wanted to be a soldier but couldn't because he had a heart condition. When Hitler came to power in Europe he was all for it, thinking that at last Germany would be known as the best country in the world. He had been a teacher but had been forced to leave teaching because of bad things that he was trying to teach to the children. He had never left America before he came to England, which happened because of a fantastic coincidence. It was that coincidence that had the whole village gasping. It was about Miss Hicks.

The police had had the whole story out of her. Miss Hicks did have a father but he was very well and living in London. Before the war started he had been a member of a political party that called itself the Union of British Fascists. In Germany, the fascists were known as Nazis and were very unpleasant people. Although the British fascist party doesn't exist anymore, some of its members such as Mr. Hicks still idolised Hitler. He had travelled to America and had met up with a group of people who thought like himself, including Mr. Mitchell. When the king had died and it was known that a coronation for the new queen would be held the next year, Miss Hicks and her father came up with a plan to "pay England back." The plan was to shoot Mr. Winston Churchill who had been a great man during the war and who, as Prime Minister, was going to take part in the coronation. Mr. Mitchell was going to do the shooting.

It was a friend of Mr. Hicks on the county council who had arranged for Mr. Mitchell to take Miss Hicks's place at our school. Those two couldn't meet in case someone saw them talking together so they had ways of keeping in touch. One of them was to leave coded messages. If Miss Hicks had something important to tell Mr. Mitchell she would ride into the village after dark and leave him a coded message in a secret place. First of all they had used a hollow in the hedge by our den. It had been Mr. Mitchell who had injured Stinky Jim, probably with the butt of his gun. It was thought he had caught Stinky searching the hedge (possibly for nuts) but when Stinky had turned and said his usual accusing, "I knows who you are. I'll tell the authorities about you." Mr. Mitchell must have thought he'd been discovered, panicked and hit him. After that Miss Hicks left the messages in a crack in the tomb in the churchyard. Then we had another shock. Mrs. Clay was also not who we thought she was. She was still

71

the lovely motherly Sunday school teacher we all liked so much but during the war she too had been involved in secret work, just like our father. Even this long after the war we were not allowed to know what it was.

The authorities in America had discovered Mr. Hicks's plan through a member of the fascist group who had been arrested. They had warned the police in London who in turn asked the local police to keep their eyes open and try to get evidence against Miss Hicks and Mr. Mitchell. Of all the people in the village only Constable Banks was allowed to know about Mrs. Clay's war work so that she could help him. It was only after Mrs. Clay had found one of their messages stuffed into the crack in the tomb and had been able to decipher it that the police were able to make their move. When Mitch and the others had left me in order to tell someone what Mr. Mitchell was doing, they had run into Mrs. Clay who got on her bicycle and rode quickly to tell Constable Banks, who raised the alarm.

Mum said later that when Mrs. Clay came to see her that Sunday after she'd talked to me about my letter she had, in a roundabout way, warned her not to get involved with Mr. Mitchell. Mum had assumed at the time that Mrs. Clay thought he was a married man.

And so it was over. Miss Hicks and her father had been arrested and would probably end up in prison. That made Johnny very happy.

It's August again now. The coronation, which we watched crowded around Doctor Simmonds's television set, was wonderful and Mr. Winston Churchill was quite safe. Cora has a new baby sister and Constable Banks has been to our house a lot. Mum calls him Maurice now, instead of Constable Banks, and he calls her by her name, Edie. We have left the village school and will be going to new schools next term. Mr. Philpot taught us for the rest of the year. He has helped me to learn sign language. Yes, I tried again. Mrs. Clay had to have a speech therapist to teach her to speak properly again and Mr. Philpot asked this lady to come to the school to give me lessons. Her name is Jane, she's not old and really nice and makes the lessons a lot of fun. She says I'm doing really well. She also helped Johnny, along with Mr. Philpot. Mr. Philpot told the class that Johnny isn't dim, he has a condition called dyslexia which means his brain mixes up words. Miss Hicks had claimed that she had been helping Johnny. Mr. Philpot was very cross to find that, far from helping him, Miss Hicks had been picking on Johnny.

Best of all, Mrs. Mason did come back to see us and she brought someone, or rather two someones, with her. They came in as if they weren't sure that they would be welcome and Granddad certainly didn't look very welcoming. They were our other grandparents, Peter Shultz's mother and father. At first our meeting was very strained and they were quite emotional to meet Mum and especially us, but in conversation Mr. Schultz mentioned he was fond of woodwork. Granddad then offered to show him his latest piece. Mr. Schultz was surprised that Granddad could still do woodwork with only one arm and was very complimentary. Off they went to the shed and the women seemed to relax. Soon Peter's mother was discussing with Gran how they had made the meat ration go round during the war and from then on we were all friends. They live in London so we don't see them very often. They have asked us to call them Oma and Opa, which is German for Granny and Granddad, even though Oma is English. They have given us photos of our father which we keep by our beds and they have given Mum the medal that he was awarded for his bravery. She didn't want to take it from them but they insisted so now it has pride of place on the sideboard in the front room next to his photo and that of Uncle Peter.

We took our eleven-plus examination in the spring. Mitch and Johnny will be going to the boys' school in Ashwood while Cora and I will be going to the girls' school in Dourwell so we will be split up. We're all sad about that, especially Mitch and me as it will be the first time in our lives that we won't be together. However, I can't help being excited at the thought that this will be a new part of our lives. We will, of course, never forget the adventure of the winter but even now, only a few months on, it feels as though it all happened ages ago, back when we were children.

****

Printed in Poland
by Amazon Fulfillment
Poland Sp. z o.o., Wrocław